DRAGON PIZZERIA

Mary Morgan

ALFRED A. KNOPF
New York

For my very own dragons: Dylan, Jere, and Jean Jacques

THIS IS A BORZOI BOOK PUBLISHED BY ALFRED A. KNOPF

Published in the United States by Alfred A. Knopf, an imprint of Random House Children's Books, a division of Random House, Inc., New York.
Knopf, Borzoi Books, and the colophon are registered trademarks of Random House, Inc.

Visit us on the Web! www.randomhouse.com/kids

Educators and librarians, for a variety of teaching tools, visit us at www.randomhouse.com/teachers

Library of Congress Cataloging-in-Publication Data
Morgan, Mary.
Dragon pizzeria / Mary Morgan. — 1st ed.
p. cm.
Summary: Two dragons, BeBop and Spike, open a pizzeria in Fairy Tale Land and deliver unique pizzas to various fairy tale characters.
ISBN 978-0-375-82309-1 (trade) — ISBN 978-0-375-92309-8 (lib. bdg.)
[1. Dragons—Fiction. 2. Pizza—Fiction. 3. Characters in literature—Fiction. 4. Nursery rhymes—Fiction.] I. Title.
PZ7.M82533Dr 2008
[E]—dc22
2007021856

MANUFACTURED IN MALAYSIA
May 2008
10 9 8 7 6 5 4 3 2

First Edition

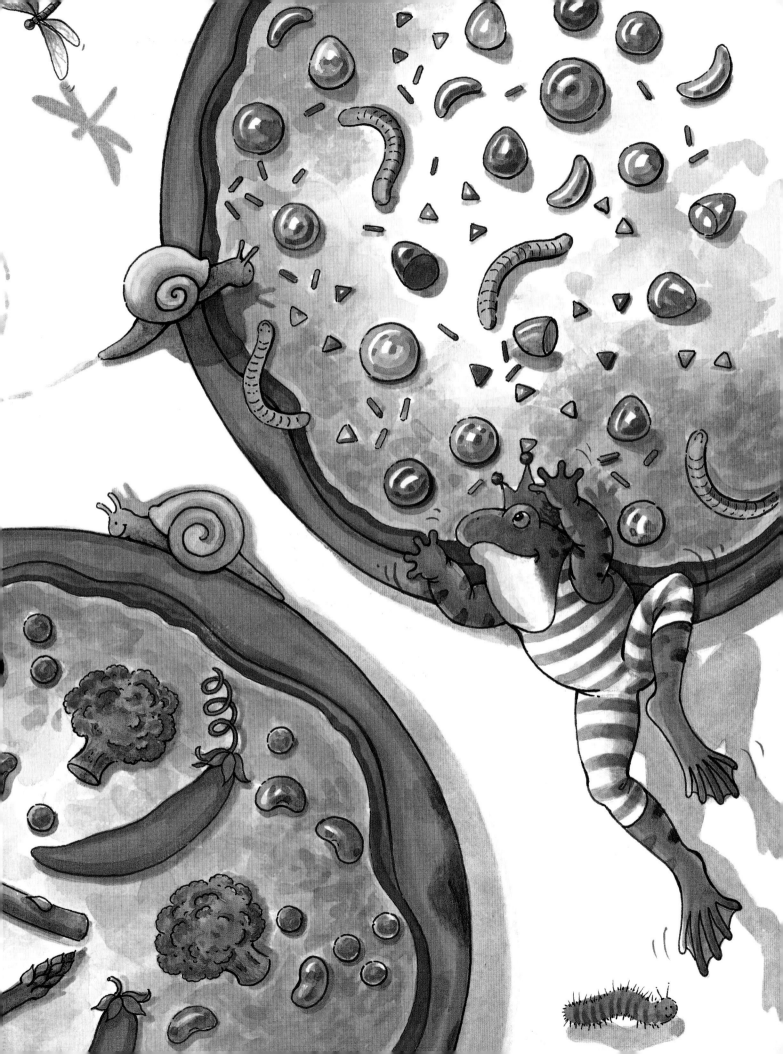

I eat my pizzas with honey.
I've done it all my life.
They do taste kind of funny,
but it keeps them on the knife.

Once upon a time, two friends decided to open a pizza shop. BeBop loved to cook. He wanted to make pizzas. Spike liked to go fast. The faster he went, the better he liked it. So he would deliver the pizzas.

We will deliver pizzas to everyone here in Fairy Tale Land!

Great idea!

Hello, Dragon Pizzeria.
This is Spike.
What would you like?

*"I would like
1 GIANT pizza,
with a topping
of magic beans.
Deliver it to
Beanstalk Castle,"
boomed a deep voice.*

Who would eat magic-bean pizza?

Spike packed the pizza in his hot-air balloon, and up and up he flew. Suddenly a huge hand came toward Spike . . .

. . . and grabbed the pizza!

Who would eat frog, snail, and green lizard-tail pizza?

Spike jumped in his rocket and delivered the pizzas.

VAROOM!

BRRIING! BRRIING!

Hello, Dragon Pizzeria.
This is Spike.
What would you like?

"I would like 3 porridge pizzas:
1 great big hot porridge pizza;
1 medium cold porridge pizza;
and 1 itty-bitty just-right
porridge pizza.
Please deliver them to
the cottage in the Wild Wood,"
said a growly voice.

Who would eat porridge pizza?

Spike roller-skated on a path through the woods—
and almost ran into a girl with golden curls.

He swerved to miss her and fell. He piled
the porridge back on the pizzas . . .

Who would eat rose-petal pizza?

Spike zoomed down the road on his unicycle,
juggling the 4 tiny pizzas.

He came to the Sweet Brier Bush.

Who would eat gingerbread pizza?

Spike sped on his skateboard to the gingerbread house,
warming the pizzas on the way.

Spike set up his high wire. He zoomed to the castle. Broooom!

Pizza Dragon! Won't you join our party? I am marrying Prince Charming today. He woke me with a kiss!

Spike delivered the pizza wedding cake, the grandest pizza that BeBop had ever baked!

Then everyone ate the cake, the most delicious pizza ever baked!

GIANT'S
BEANSTALK
CASTLE

SLEEPING BEAUTY'S
CASTLE

THE THORN
BUSH FOREST

THE THREE BEARS'
COTTAGE

Fairy Tale Land

The Frog Prince

DRAGON
PIZZERIA

DRAGON
MOUNTAIN

Hansel
and
Gretel

THE BLACK FOREST

WITCH'S
GINGERBREAD HOUSE

THE WILD WOOD

THUMBELINA'S SWEET BRIER BUSH

THE ENCHANTED
GARDEN